Order this book online at www.trafford.com
or email orders@trafford.com

Most Trafford titles are also available at major online book retailers.

 www.trafford.com

North America & international
toll-free: 844 688 6899 (USA & Canada)
fax: 812 355 4082

Our mission is to efficiently provide the world's finest, most comprehensive book publishing service, enabling every author to experience success. To find out how to publish your book, your way, and have it available worldwide, visit us online at www.trafford.com

Because of the dynamic nature of the Internet, any web addresses or links contained in this book may have changed since publication and may no longer be valid. The views expressed in this work are solely those of the author and do not necessarily reflect the views of the publisher, and the publisher hereby disclaims any responsibility for them.

Any people depicted in stock imagery provided by Getty Images are models, and such images are being used for illustrative purposes only.
Certain stock imagery © Getty Images.

ISBN: 978-1-6987-1115-7 (sc)
ISBN: 978-1-6987-1114-0 (e)

Print information available on the last page.

Trafford rev. 02/17/2022

The Adventures of

Spotty
and
Sunny

Book 8: A Fun Learning Series for kids

It is Magical

Author/ Pharmacist
Saisnath Baijoo.

Grandpa runs to his car, "Kids, wait here. I am going to my car to get a basket of food. We are at Everglades Park. We will have lunch here."

Davin raises his hands, "Oh my! Grandpa brings us in the middle of nowhere."

Dominic shows a sad face, "Aww man. I prefer to play games on my computer at home. There is no Wi-Fi or internet here."

Jas, Dominic, and Davin look bored. Jordi jokes quietly, "A boring day with Grandpa." Everyone laughs.

It is a beautiful, sunny day at the park. Grandpa returns quickly. He is short of breath and tired. "Kids, we are here to have fun. Who is hungry?"

Everyone is sad but hungry. Jas looks around, "You know this place is awesome and I love it. My pet rabbit and Cuddles can play. There is a playground and a beach."

"Look kids, I have your favorite yummy foods. There are blueberry pancakes with syrup. I made your favorite roti or Indian bread with fried potatoes, ham, and cheese. I have chocolate cereal. I have chocolate milk and water." Grandpa placed all the food on a cloth on the ground for a picnic under a big, shady tree. Everyone grabs food and eats.

Davin says. "Thank you, Grandpa, for lunch."

Grandpa smiles, "Welcome my son. Look, there are many colorful birds singing on this tall tree."

Davin says. "Look, the red and yellow birds are singing sweet."

Grandpa adds. "I think the black and white birds are singing sweeter."

Dominic points. "No, no. My blue, gray and brown bird is singing the sweetest. He is the king. He has a crown on his head."

Suddenly, Jordi stands and points to the skies joyfully. "Look, I can see my friends coming this way. It is Miss Can, the pelican, and Mr. Owl." Jordi jumps. He spills all the milk.

Davin jokes, "How do you know them?"

Jordi says happily, "Oh yes, I remember them from my dream."

Jas laughs loudly, "Really, from your dream, you say?"

Everyone laughs at Jordi.

Miss Can and Mr. Owl lands near them. She hugs Jordi. "Hello again, my friend. How are you? Are you going to sing today?"Miss Can points to the rainbow-colored bus coming into the park. "Look Spotty, Sunny, school friends, and family will here soon. It is a school Christmas celebration at Everglades Park."

Jordi smiles. "It must be magical. My fairy mother has magical powers. Now everyone in the Everglades can talk. They can walk or swim in land and water."

Miss Can and Mr. Owl flap their big wings and sing. "We are the Sky Patrol teachers from Everglades school. We saved Spotty's life when he was a baby."

Everyone is more confused.

Their many questions are interrupted by loud music coming from the school bus. On the rainbow-colored bus is a big, red sign, that says Everglades school. The students are singing and clapping loudly. "The wheel on the bus goes round and round, round and round all through the park. If you're happy and you know it clap your hands."

Mr. Owl turns his big eyes all around his head to Grandpa. "Can the kids come? We are having a Christmas party."

Grandpa says. "Yes, go. Have fun." Everyone walks towards the bus.

The bus stops. First exits the marching band playing music.

Miss Can puffs her chest and salutes. "Here comes our famous marching parade. First, our senior class. We have the Native American Indians in their traditional wear followed complete by our Hispanic kids. Then, followed by East Indian and Chinese kids. There are kids from South Africa, Japan, Trinidad, and Tobago in the Everglades school."

Mr. Owl speaks proudly. Here comes our teachers, s Mr. Tam with his magical tambourine. Mrs. Claws with her guitar. Miss Snapper, our music teacher. Mr. Liz with his magical flute. Next, our lovable junior class. Our popular students Sunny and Spotty with Mom and Dad. Mr. Slo, the turtle and two baby turtles, Dolph, the dolphin and three baby dolphins and our four little piggies."

Drums play until everyone is standing at attention outside the bus.

Everyone claps, Miss Can and Mr. Owl walk towards the parade. "Kids come and join the fun." Jordi, Dominic, Jas, Davin, Cuddles, and pet rabbit all follow them. They are guided to seats placed for everyone. Every seat has many paint brushes, drawing papers, and colored paints.

Mrs. Snapper speaks. "Kids, I want you to paint a beautiful scenery. You are surrounded by nature. On my left, you have a beach and mountains. On my right, you have trees, animals, and birds."

Sitting in the front row is Jas, Miss Piggy number one and Mr. Slo, the baby turtle

Jas draws slow. Miss Piggy number one draws slower. Mr. Slo draws the slowest.

Spotty paints fast. Davin paints faster. Sunny paints the fastest.

Jordi smiles, "Surprises are magical."

Everyone finishes their drawing. They run around
the park to the beat of many drums.

Everyone is tired after running. They return to their seats.
On their seats are slices of pizza, a fruit drink and a gift
wrapped present. All the children are surprised and happy.

The sun is setting. It is getting dark. Mother Fairy appears and the skies are filled with fireworks.

"It is really magical." shouts Jordi. Everyone gathers around for hugs and group selfies to capture many magical moments.

Davin asks Miss Can. "Where is my grandpa?

She replies with a smile. "He is sleeping in his car."

Suddenly everyone hears the jolly sounds. "Ho, ho, ho." They look up in the star filled sky.

Sunny says, "It is Santa with his reindeers. It is magical.

Thank you for your order on sbaijao.com
Text me at (786) 223-2563
Follow me on Facebook, Instagram, and Twitter

Printed in the United States
by Baker & Taylor Publisher Services